THE FIRST MOON LANDING

BY PATRICIA HUTCHISON

Published by The Child's World®
1980 Lookout Drive • Mankato, MN 56003-1705
800-599-READ • www.childsworld.com

Acknowledgments
The Child's World®: Mary Berendes, Publishing Director
Red Line Editorial: Design, editorial direction, and production
Photographs ©: Neil A. Armstrong/National Aeronautics and Space Administration, cover, 1, 14, 16; National Aeronautics and Space Administration, 4, 7, 10, 12, 18, 20, 21; Bettmann/Corbis, 6; Shutterstock Images, 9

Copyright © 2016 by The Child's World®
All rights reserved. No part of this book may be reproduced or utilized in any form or by any means without written permission from the publisher.

ISBN 9781634074766

LCCN 2015946220

Printed in the United States of America
Mankato, MN
December, 2015
PA02280

ABOUT THE AUTHOR

Patricia Hutchison, as a young girl, was one of the half-billion people who was awed while watching the lunar landing on television. In the classroom for more than 30 years, her favorite subject to teach was science. On clear nights, you might find her gazing through her telescope at the moon and beyond.

TABLE OF CONTENTS

Chapter 1
WE HAVE LIFTOFF!....................... 5

Chapter 2
THE *EAGLE* HAS LANDED 11

Chapter 3
HEADING HOME............................ 19

Glossary 22
Source Notes 23
To Learn More 24
Index 24

Chapter 1

WE HAVE LIFTOFF!

"Ignition sequence start . . . 6, 5, 4, 3, 2, 1, 0 . . . All engines running. Liftoff! We have a liftoff."[1] A huge fireball blasted out of the rocket. Large clouds of smoke surrounded it. The thunderous roar shook the ground miles away. Slowly, the rocket lifted from Earth. Moments later, it was a speck in the sky. A long trail of smoke followed it. The Saturn V rocket was carrying the Apollo 11 crew into space.

It was 9:32 a.m. on July 16, 1969. Eight years earlier, President Kennedy had made a challenge. He wanted the United States to put a man on the moon before 1970. Would Kennedy's dream come true?

The Saturn V rocket was a 363-foot (110-m) giant. It needed 7.5 million pounds (33 million **newtons**) of **thrust** to escape Earth's gravity. Three astronauts sat aboard the spacecraft at the top of the rocket. This was not the first space mission for these

◀ **The Apollo 11 crew takes off from Kennedy Space Center in Florida.**

▲ Michael Collins sits in the Command Module during a training session in June 1969.

men. Neil Armstrong, Buzz Aldrin, and Michael Collins were experts at piloting rockets. Now the men were looking down on Earth. They were flying 120 miles (193 km) above the planet. Their ship cruised at an amazing 17,400 miles per hour (28,000 km/h). Aldrin felt a sense of calm come over him.

The astronauts spent the next few hours **orbiting** Earth. They circled the planet one and a half times. Aldrin said, "We've got the continent of Africa . . . facing toward us right now . . .

everything's getting smaller and smaller."[2] The men took pictures and sent them back to Earth. The pictures showed a mostly brown Africa. The continent was green in the middle, under some white clouds. More clouds swirled over the blue seas. The South Pole was covered in white ice.

The astronauts flew higher. The blue band of Earth's atmosphere stood out against the blackness of space. The

▲ **Earth floats in space as the Apollo 11 astronauts speed toward the moon.**

rocket's engine fired again. The spacecraft escaped the pull of Earth's gravity. The men were hurling toward the moon at 24,400 miles per hour (39,300 km/h).

Their spacecraft had three parts. The first part was the cone-shaped Command Module, also known as the *Columbia*. It was about as big as a car. This small cabin would be the astronauts' home for eight days. All three of them would eat, sleep, and even go to the bathroom there. The second part of the ship was the Service Module. It was for power and storage. The ship's third part was called the *Eagle*. This was the **Lunar Module** that would land on the moon.

The Saturn V rocket was now out of fuel. It separated from the ship and floated off into space. But the Apollo 11 crew continued speeding toward the moon. By about 9:00 p.m., the men were tired. They slept, floating weightlessly in the cabin.

By the morning of the third day, the crew was preparing to orbit the moon. They could see it up close. Armstrong said, "The view of the moon that we've been having recently is really spectacular . . . part of it is in complete shadow, and part of it's in earth-shine. It's a view worth the price of the trip."[3]

PARTS OF THE APOLLO 11 SPACECRAFT

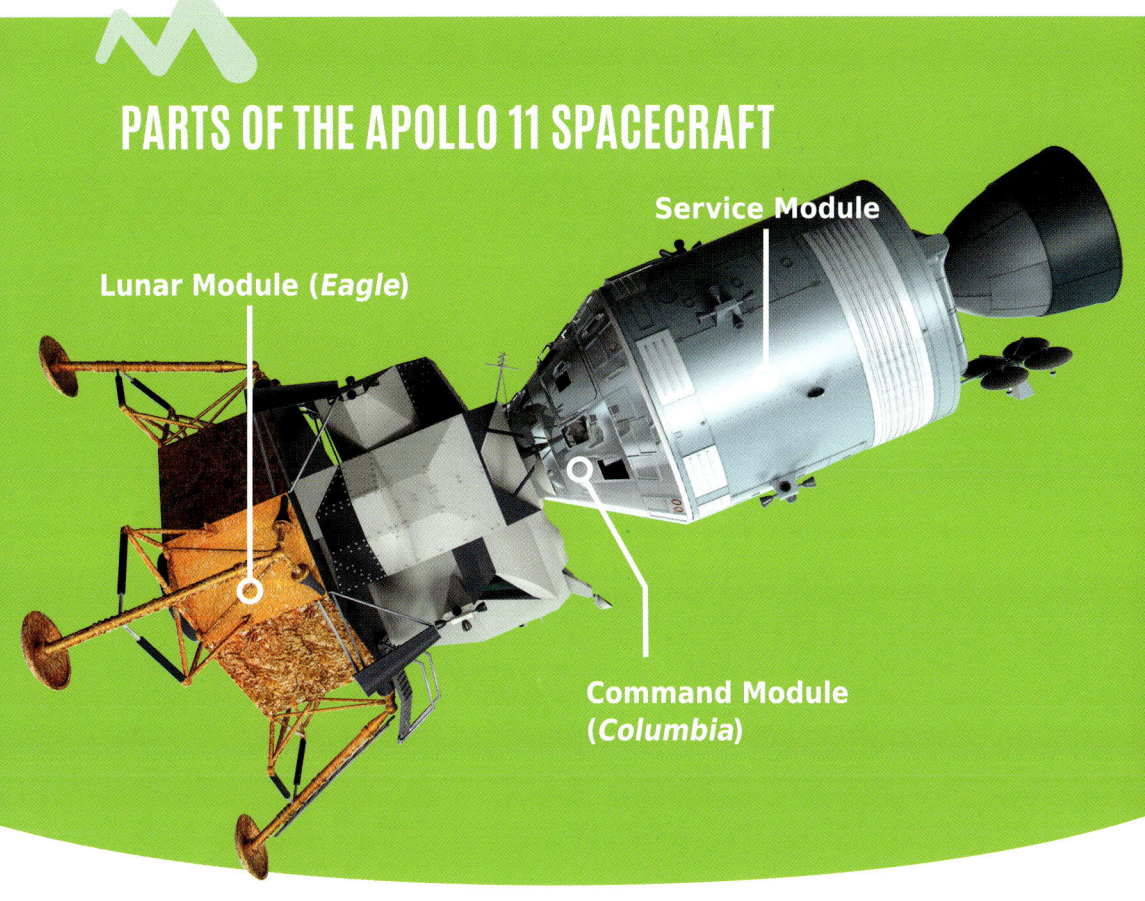

On the fourth day, Armstrong and Aldrin climbed into the *Eagle*. Collins stayed alone in the *Columbia*. He pressed a button, and the spaceship sprung into two parts. The *Columbia* and the Service Module remained in orbit. The *Eagle* spun toward the lunar surface. Collins later wrote that the bug-shaped *Eagle* was "the weirdest looking **contraption** I have ever seen in the sky, but it would prove its worth."[4]

Chapter 2

THE *EAGLE* HAS LANDED

Moving closer to the moon's surface in the *Eagle*, Armstrong saw huge boulders in the landing site. He knew the *Eagle* could be destroyed if it smashed into the rocks. The captain took control of his ship. He steered the *Eagle* forward. They sailed over the rocks.

Alarms began to buzz and ring. Sixty seconds worth of fuel remained. The astronauts had reached the "dead man's zone." If the *Eagle* ran out of fuel, they would crash into the moon's surface. Armstrong continued on. Soon, only 30 seconds worth of fuel was left. Aldrin looked at the **Abort** button. Armstrong's heart started pounding. At 4:18 p.m., the spacecraft settled down with a jolt. It felt like a jet plane landing on a runway.

"The *Eagle* has landed," Armstrong said calmly.[5]

◀ The *Eagle* makes its descent toward the moon.

▲ **Earth sits on the horizon of the moon.**

From Earth, Mission Control replied, "Roger . . . we copy you on the ground. You've got a bunch of guys about to turn blue. We're breathing again. Thanks a lot."[6]

Aldrin shook Armstrong's hand. They had done it! Their ship was on the surface of the moon.

First, the astronauts prepared the *Eagle* for liftoff from the moon. They wanted to be able to take off right away if there was an emergency. The men were supposed to sleep before they went out to explore the moon's surface. But they were too excited to wait. Five hours ahead of schedule, they put on their heavy space suits. Armstrong opened the hatch and squeezed through. He moved slowly down the ladder.

What would it be like to walk on the moon? More than 500 million people wondered as they watched the events on TV. At 10:56 p.m., Armstrong pressed his left boot into the powdery surface of the moon. He said, "That's one small step for a man, one giant leap for mankind."[7]

At the bottom of the ladder, he looked around. The moon looked like a beautiful desert. Shuffling cautiously away from the *Eagle*, Armstrong took out a small sack. He collected a sample of lunar surface material and put it in his pocket. If they had to abort the mission, scientists would at least have some moon rocks to study.

Next, it was Aldrin's turn. He jumped off the ladder and joined Armstrong on the surface. "Beautiful view!" he said.[8] The men felt nearly weightless. Aldrin took small steps at first, testing out his moon legs. Then he tried hopping like a kangaroo. Armstrong flapped his arms to see if he would lift off. He didn't. He wasn't light enough. Soon, Aldrin was jogging around. He looked like a slow-motion sports replay. "Isn't it fun?" Armstrong asked his partner.[9]

The moon is much smaller than Earth. The curved lunar horizon seemed very close. The surface was bright, but the sky was completely black. The astronauts could not see any stars. There was only one object in the sky. It was the blue and white Earth.

It was time to get down to business. Staying close to the *Eagle*, the men began to explore. They found rock fragments covering the moon's surface. These fragments were like fine sand. There were also pebbles and some boulders. "The surface is fine and powdery. . . . I can kick it up loosely with my toe," Armstrong said.[10]

The astronauts set up some experiments. Aldrin drove a pole into the surface. There was a roll of foil on it to catch particles of **solar** wind that blow through space. Scientists hoped this would tell them how the Sun and planets were formed. Next, the men planted an American flag into the surface of the moon.

Then it was time for a phone call. President Richard Nixon was one of the millions of people watching on TV. Mission Control told the astronauts that the president wanted to speak to them. "Because of what you have done, the heavens have become part of man's world," Nixon told them by telephone. "All the people on this Earth are truly one."

◀ **Buzz Aldrin climbs down the ladder as he prepares to set foot on the moon.**

"Thank you, Mr. President," said Armstrong. "It's an honor for us to be able to participate here today."[11]

The experiments continued. Armstrong scooped up rocks and soil and put them in sealed boxes. Aldrin set up a device that would record moonquakes. He also set up a laser-reflector. This instrument would measure the distances between the moon and the Earth. Soon they had completed all of the tasks on their list. After two amazing hours of walking on the moon, the astronauts climbed back into the *Eagle*.

◀ **Aldrin sets up scientific equipment as the *Eagle* sits in the background.**

Chapter 3

HEADING HOME

Safely back in the *Eagle*, the men took off their space suits. They noticed a strange odor. Four-billion-year-old moon dust had stuck to their boots. Aldrin said it smelled like gunpowder. Armstrong compared it to wet ashes in a fireplace. Mission control had questions about the surface of the moon. The men answered them. Finally, it was time to try to sleep. Aldrin curled up on the floor of the *Eagle*. Armstrong made himself a hammock. After all the excitement of the day, sleep did not come easily.

The next morning, July 21, it was time to leave the moon. But as the men prepared for takeoff, they discovered a big problem. They could not fire the engine. One of the switches was broken. Mission Control tried to fix it from Earth, but they had no luck. How would the men get back to the *Columbia*? As a last resort, Aldrin jammed a pen into the **breaker**. The engine ignited! The *Eagle* lifted off. It began its journey back to the *Columbia*, where Collins was still orbiting the moon.

◀ The *Eagle* makes its way back up to the *Columbia*.

▲ **The Apollo 11 astronauts get into a raft after exiting the *Columbia*.**

The landing gear of the *Eagle* stayed behind on the moon's surface. There was a **plaque** attached to it. It read, "Here men from the planet Earth first set foot upon the moon July 1969, A.D. We came in peace for all mankind."[12]

Aldrin and Armstrong docked with Collins in the *Columbia*. Collins breathed a sigh of relief.

The next morning, the Service Module fired up. The astronauts started their journey back to Earth. On July 23, Earth's gravity grabbed the ship and began to pull them homeward. When they reached Earth's atmosphere, they detached the Service Module. The *Columbia* continued speeding toward Earth. Three giant parachutes burst open, slowing it down. At 12:51 p.m. on July 24, the *Columbia* made a huge splash in the Pacific

20

Ocean near Hawaii. The tiny ship bobbed on its side and then turned right side up.

The hatch of the spacecraft opened. The astronauts were safe! President Kennedy's dream was now a reality. Soon, President Nixon greeted the men. He said, "This is the greatest week in the history of the world. . . . We can reach for the stars."[13]

▲ **President Nixon met with the astronauts after they returned to Earth.**

GLOSSARY

abort (uh-BORT): Abort means to put an end to something before it is finished. The astronauts were prepared in case they had to abort the mission.

breaker (BRAY-kur): A breaker is an electrical switch. When an electrical current gets overloaded, the circuit breaker will stop the flow of electricity.

contraption (kun-TRAP-shun): A contraption is a device or gadget. The *Eagle* was an interesting contraption.

ignition (ig-NISH-un): Ignition is the lighting of a fuel mixture to cause a fire. Apollo 11 began its ignition sequence and then blasted off.

lunar (LOO-nur): Lunar means having to do with the moon. The lunar surface is full of craters.

newtons (NOO-tunz): Newtons are units that measure force. One pound of force is equal to approximately 4.4 newtons.

orbiting (OR-bit-ing): Orbiting means moving in a circle around an object in space. The Apollo 11 astronauts were orbiting the moon in the *Columbia*.

plaque (PLAK): A plaque is a special sign used as a marker. A plaque on the landing gear told when the astronauts landed on the moon.

solar (SOL-uhr): Solar means having to do with the Sun. The foil in the experiment picked up solar particles.

thrust (THRUST): Thrust is the force produced by a propeller rocket engine that drives a rocket upward. It took millions of pounds of thrust to lift Apollo 11 off the ground.

SOURCE NOTES

1. Brian Dunbar. "Sounds from Apollo 11." *NASA*. NASA, n.d. Web. 28 May 2015.

2. "Apollo 11 Flight Journal." *NASA*. NASA, 16 Feb. 2012. Web. 28 May 2015.

3. "Apollo 11 Mission Logs." *NASA*. NASA, n.d. Web. 28 May 2015.

4. "July 20, 1969: One Giant Leap For Mankind." *NASA*. NASA, 14 Jul. 2014. Web. 28 May 2015.

5. "EP-72 Log of Apollo 11." *NASA*. NASA, n.d. Web. 28 May 2015.

6. "Apollo Expeditions to the Moon: A Yellow Caution Light." *NASA*. NASA, n.d. Web. 28 May 2015.

7. "EP-72 Log of Apollo 11." *NASA*. NASA, n.d. Web. 28 May 2015.

8. "Wide Awake on the Sea of Tranquility." *NASA*. NASA, 9 Jul. 2014. Web. 28 May 2015.

9. Buzz Aldrin and Malcolm McConnell. *Men from Earth*. New York: Bantam, 1989. Print. 239.

10. "One Small Step." *NASA*. NASA, 5 May 2015. Web. 28 May 2015.

11. "Man Walks on Another World." *National Geographic*. National Geographic Society, n.d. Web. 28 May 2015.

12. "July 20, 1969: One Giant Leap For Mankind." *NASA*. NASA, 14 Jul. 2014. Web. 28 May 2015.

13. "EP-72 Log of Apollo 11." *NASA*. NASA, n.d. Web. 28 May 2015.

TO LEARN MORE

Books

Floca, Brian. *Moonshot: The Flight of Apollo 11*. New York: Atheneum, 2009.

Stone, Jerry. *One Small Step: Celebrating the First Men on the Moon*. New York: Flash Point, 2009.

Thimmesh, Catherine. *Team Moon: How 400,000 People Landed Apollo 11 on the Moon*. Boston: Houghton Mifflin, 2006.

Web Sites

Visit our Web site for links about the first moon landing: childsworld.com/links

Note to Parents, Teachers, and Librarians: We routinely verify our Web links to make sure they are safe and active sites. So encourage your readers to check them out!

INDEX

Aldrin, Buzz, 6, 9, 11, 12, 13, 15, 17, 19, 20

Apollo 11, 5, 8

Armstrong, Neil, 6, 8, 9, 11, 12, 13, 15, 17, 19, 20

Collins, Michael, 6, 9, 19, 20

Columbia, 8, 9, 19, 20

Eagle, 8, 9, 11, 12, 13, 15, 17, 19, 20

experiments, 15, 17

Kennedy, John F., 5, 21

Mission Control, 12, 15, 19

Nixon, Richard, 15, 21

plaque, 20

Saturn V rocket, 5, 8

Service Module, 8, 9, 20